Moonthief

For Tom and Caroline – RMcG
For Marcia with love – PD

KINGFISHER
An imprint of Kingfisher Publications Plc
New Penderel House, 283-288 High Holborn, London WC1V 7HZ
www.kingfisherpub.com

First published by Kingfisher 2002
First published in paperback by Kingfisher 2004
10 9 8 7 6 5 4 3 2 1

Text copyright © Roger McGough 2002
Illustrations copyright © Penny Dann 2002

A CIP catalogue record for this book is available from the British Library.

ISBN 0 7534 0900 3

Printed in Singapore
1TR/TWP/CG(CG)/170NYA

Moonthief

Roger McGough

Illustrated by Penny Dann

KINGFISHER

"Look, there's a new
moon out tonight,"
said Bobby.

"I wonder what they
did with the old one,"
said Betty.

"But how did it get there?"

"I stole it."

"Moon

thief!"

"I hitched a ride on a shooting star and while the man-in-the-moon had his back turned, I blew it up with a bicycle pump and floated back down to earth."

"Phew!" said Betty, her eyes
wide open. "But why?"
"To give to you."
She smiled mischievously.
"Silly Bear, what could I
do with an old moon?"

"You could take it
to bed with you,"
said Bobby.

"Instead of
my teddy?"

"You could train it
to fetch your slippers."

"You can't teach an old moon new tricks."

"You could keep goldfish in it . . ."

"GOLDFISH!"

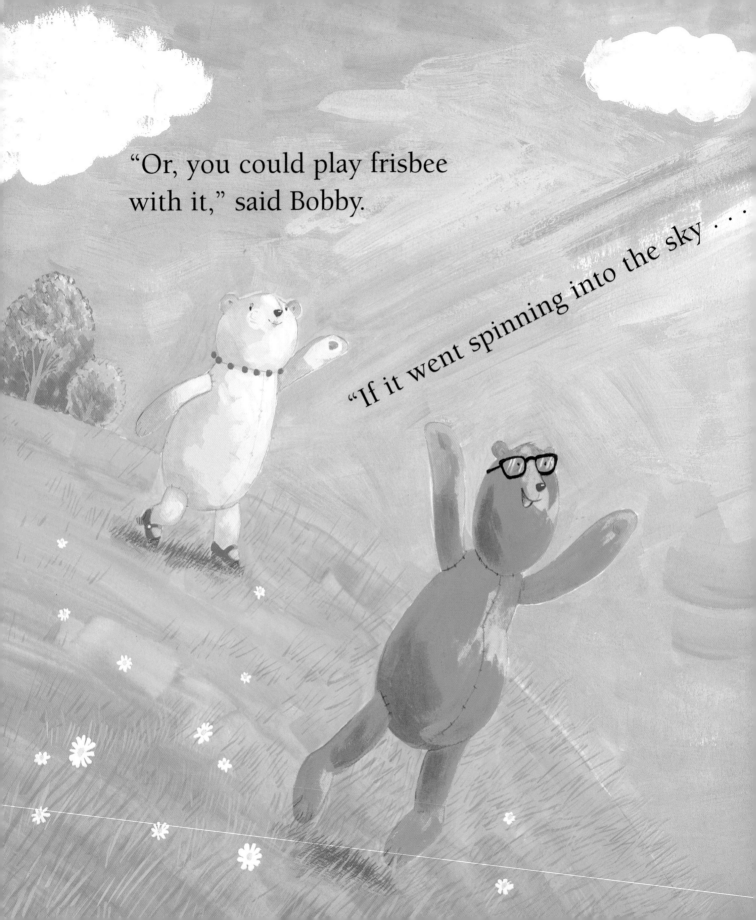

"Or, you could play frisbee with it," said Bobby.

"If it went spinning into the sky . . .

it might never come back," said Betty.

"You could lead the big
parade with it," said Bobby.
"Dumpity, Dumpity, Dum.
Dumpity, Dumpity—"

"It wouldn't be fair to beat the moon,"
said Betty.
"Dum!" said Bobby, and then thought
for a while.

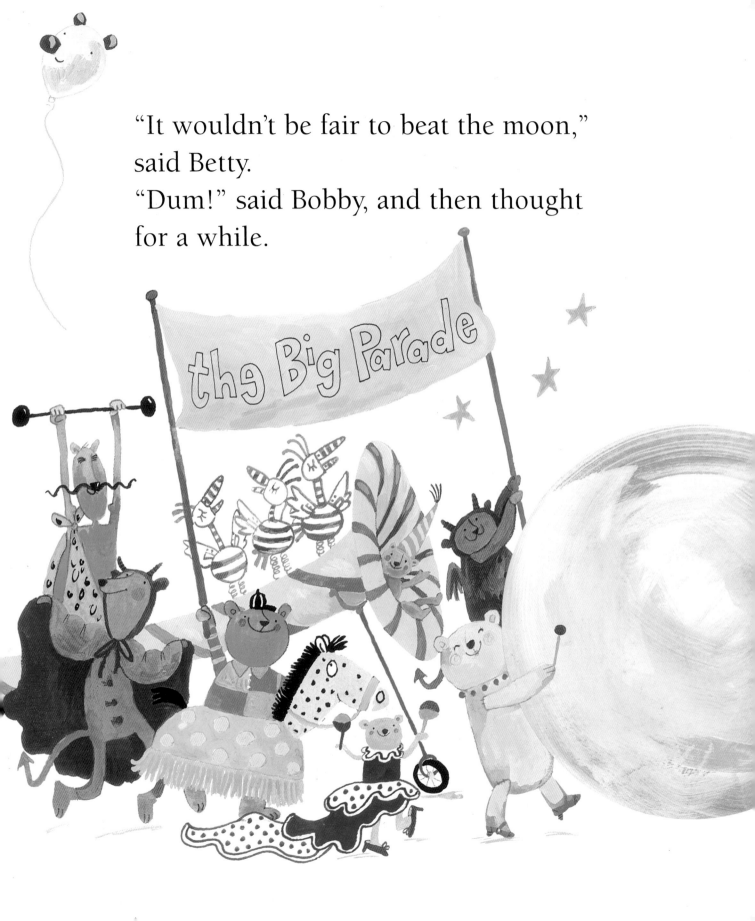

"You could use it as a silver tray
and serve chilled drinks upon it."
"Mmm . . ." mmmed Betty.

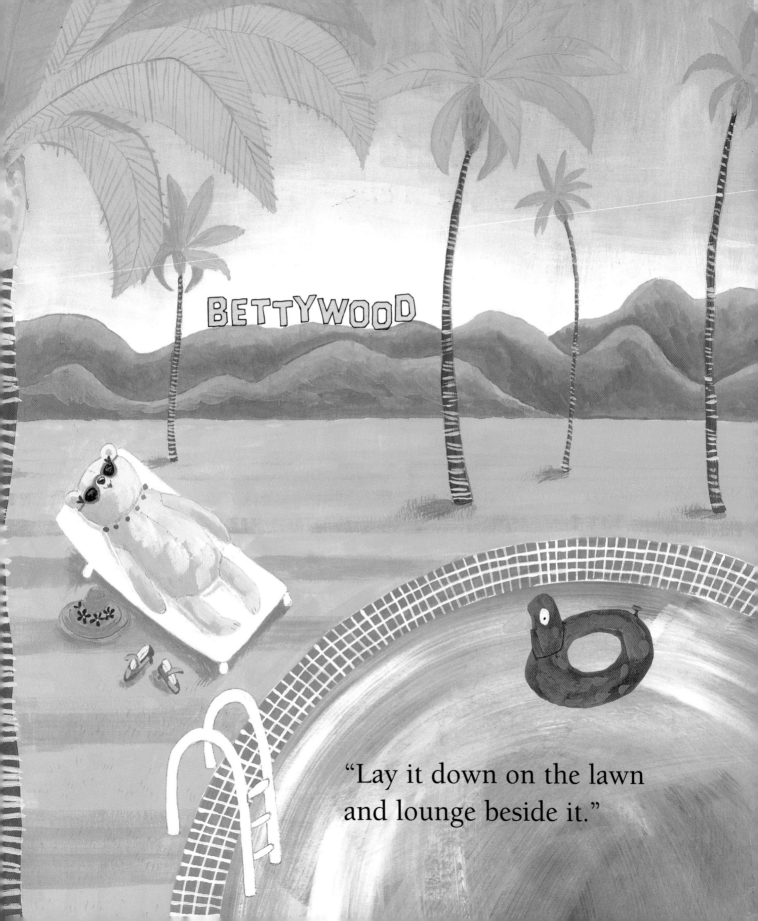

"Lay it down on the lawn
and lounge beside it."

"Or, you could hang it up in the bathroom when you're fixing your hair with the pink ribbons I just knew would come in useful."

Betty reflected on the idea.

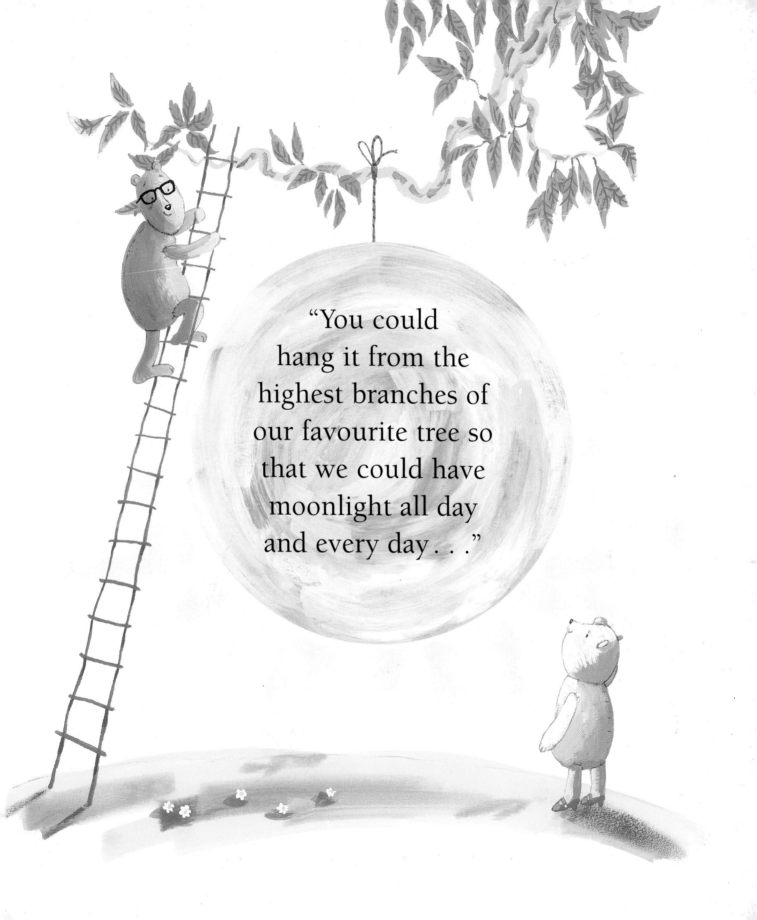

"You could
hang it from the
highest branches of
our favourite tree so
that we could have
moonlight all day
and every day . . ."

"Or," said Bobby, becoming really excited now . . .

"You could score goals with it

play tenpin bowls with it

go ice-skating on it

trampolining on it . . .

or . . .
or . . .
or . . .

you could be the first
lady bear on the moon!"

Betty interrupted.
"But what about the man?"

"What man?"

"The man-in-the-moon,
silly. Does he know you've
stolen it?"

"I didn't actually *steal* it,"
said Bobby. "I just borrowed
it for a few hours."

Betty looked at him sternly.
"I think you should put
it back where it belongs,
don't you?"

"I suppose so," said Bobby,
shrugging his shoulders.

Then, taking off his glasses
and polishing them with a
dock leaf, he said quietly,
"I just wanted to give you
the most brilliant present
in the whole universe."

"Oh, you Silly Bear," said Betty,
and taking hold of his paw
gave it a big squeeze.

I don't want the moon, or the sun,
or the stars, because . . .

of all the bears
in this wide, wide,
moonlit world . . ."

Bobby began to blush . . .

and blush, and blush, and blush, and blush . . .

"All I want is . . .